D0100301

To my mummy

love from

....

First published in paperback in Great Britain by HarperCollins Children's Books in 2006

3 5 7 9 10 8 6 4 2

ISBN-13: 978-0-00-720599-8
ISBN-10: 0-00-720599-6

HarperCollins Children's Books is a division of HarperCollins Publishers Ltd.
Text and illustrations copyright © HarperCollins Publishers Ltd 2006

A CIP catalogue record for this title is available from the British Library. All rights reserved.
No part of this publication may be reproduced, stored in a retrieval system or transmitted in any form
or by any means, electronic, mechanical, photocopying, recording or otherwise, without the prior permission
of HarperCollins Publishers Ltd, 77-85 Fulham Palace Road, Hammersmith, London W6 8JB.

Visit our website at: www.harpercollinschildrensbooks.co.uk

Printed and bound in China

Why I Love My Mummy

Illustrated by Daniel Howarth

HarperCollins *Children's Books*

I love my mummy because...

she holds my hand.

I love my mummy because...

she takes me to nice places.

I love my mummy because...

she plays with me.

I love my mummy because...

she helps me.

I love my mummy because...

she teaches me.

I love my mummy because...

she is beautiful.

I love my mummy because...

she kisses me better.

I love my mummy because...

she feeds me.

I love my mummy because...

she smells nice.

I love my mummy because...

she gives me a bath.

I love my mummy because...

she sings to me.

I love my mummy because...

she always hugs me.

I love my mummy because...

she helps me sleep at night.

Everyone loves their mummy –

especially...

ME!

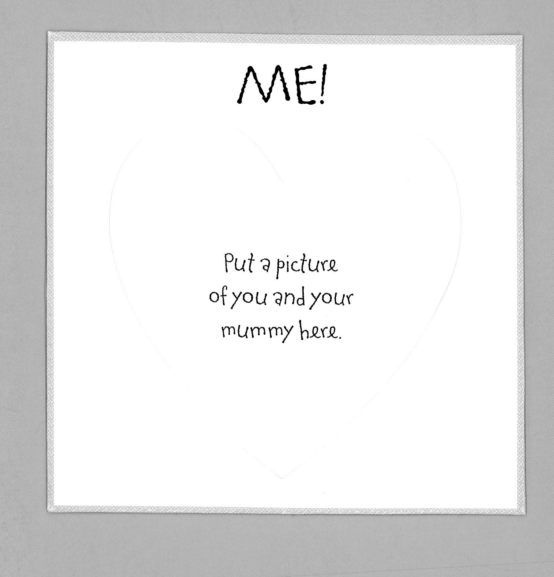

Put a picture
of you and your
mummy here.